ALFIE

Alfie's Feet

19

For Edward and Catherine

Other titles in the Alfie series:

Alfie Gets in First
Alfie Gives a Hand
An Evening at Alfie's
Alfie and the Birthday Surprise
Alfie Wins a Prize
Alfie and the Big Boys
Alfie Weather
Alfie's World
Annie Rose is my Little Sister
Rhymes for Annie Rose
The Big Alfie and Annie Rose Storybook
The Big Alfie Out of Doors Storybook

ALFIE'S FEET
A RED FOX BOOK 978 1 862 30944 9

First published in Great Britain by The Bodley Head, an imprint of Random House Children's Books
A Random House Group Company

The Bodley Head edition published 1982
Red Fox edition first published 1993
This edition with CD published 2010

1 3 5 7 9 10 8 6 4 2

Copyright © Shirley Hughes, 1982

The right of Shirley Hughes to be identified as the author and illustrator of this work has been asserted
in accordance with the Copyright, Designs and Patents Act 1988.

Red Fox Books are published by Random House Children's Books, 61–63 Uxbridge Road, London W5 5SA

www.kidsatrandomhouse.co.uk
www.rbooks.co.uk

Addresses for companies within The Random House Group Limited can be found at: www.randomhouse.co.uk/offices.htm

THE RANDOM HOUSE GROUP Limited Reg. No. 954009

A CIP catalogue record for this book is available from the British Library.

Printed in China

ALFIE

Alfie's Feet

Shirley Hughes

Red Fox

This little pig went to market,

This little pig stayed at home,

This little pig had roast beef,

This little pig had none,

And this little pig cried, Wee-wee-wee-wee-wee,

I can't find my way home.

Alfie had a little sister called Annie Rose.
Alfie's feet were quite big. Annie Rose's feet
were rather small. They were all soft and pink
underneath. Alfie knew a game he could play
with Annie Rose, counting her toes.

Annie Rose had lots of different ways of getting about. She went forwards, crawling,

and backwards, on her behind,

and she liked to slide
about very fast on her potty,

skidding round and round
on the floor and in and out
of the table legs.

Annie Rose had
some new red shoes.

She could walk in them
a bit, if she was pushing her
little cart or holding on to
someone's hand.

When they went out, Annie Rose wore her
red shoes and Alfie wore his old brown ones.
Mum usually helped him put them on, because
he wasn't very good at doing up the laces yet.

If it had been raining Alfie
liked to go stamping about in
mud and walking through puddles,

splish, splash, SPLOSH!

Then his shoes got rather wet.

So did his socks,

and so did his feet.

So one Saturday morning Alfie and Mum went to
a big shop in the High Street.

They bought a pair of shiny new yellow boots
for Alfie to wear when he went stamping about
in mud and walking through puddles. Alfie was
very pleased. He carried them home himself in a
cardboard box.

When they got in, Alfie sat down at once and unwrapped his new boots. He put them on all by himself and walked about in them,

stamp! stamp! stamp!

He went into the kitchen to show Mum and Dad and Annie Rose, stamping his feet all the way, stamp! stamp! stamp!

The boots were very smart
and shiny but they felt funny.

Alfie wanted to go out again right away. So he put on his mac, and Dad took his book and his newspaper and they went off to the park.

Alfie stamped in a lot of mud and walked through a lot of puddles, splish, splash, SPLOSH! He frightened some sparrows who were having a bath. He even frightened two big ducks. They went hurrying back to their pond, walking with their feet turned in.

Alfie looked down at his feet. They still
felt funny. They kept turning outwards.
Dad was sitting on a bench. They both
looked at Alfie's feet.

Suddenly Alfie knew what was wrong!

Dad lifted Alfie on to the bench beside him and helped him to take off each boot and put it on the other foot. And when Alfie stood down again his feet didn't feel a bit funny any more.

After tea Mum painted a big black R on to
one of Alfie's boots and a big black L on the
other to help Alfie remember which boot was
which. The R was for Right foot and the
L was for Left foot. The black paint wore off
in the end and the boots stopped being new
and shiny, but Alfie usually did remember to
get them on the proper way round after that.
They felt much better when he went stamping
about in mud and walking through puddles.

And, of course, Annie Rose made such a fuss about Alfie having new boots that she had to have a pair of her own to go stamping about in too, splish, splash, SPLOSH!